The Mouse Family

By Andrew Clements • Illustrated by Simon Galkin

LITTLE SIMON

New York   London   Toronto   Sydney   Singapore

LITTLE SIMON

An imprint of Simon & Schuster Children's Publishing Division

1230 Avenue of the Americas

New York, New York 10020

Text and illustrations copyright © 2000 by Simon & Schuster, Inc. Cover illustration by Alison Winfield.

The names and depictions of Raggedy Ann and Raggedy Andy are trademarks of Simon & Schuster, Inc.

Manufactured in the United States of America

First Edition

2 4 6 8 10 9 7 5 3 1

ISBN 0-689-83244-3

One night in the early springtime, the dolls were in their beds. It was very quiet in the nursery. Except for one tiny sound.

Sniff, sniffity, sniff.

"What's that?" Raggedy Andy whispered to Little Brown Bear.

Little Brown Bear said, "I can't tell. It's too dark."

Raggedy Ann sat up, wide awake. She heard it too.

Sniff, sniffity, sniff.

"Let's go take a look," said Raggedy Ann.

The dolls followed the sound. It came from behind the toy chest. Without making any noise, they pulled the chest away from the wall.

"Look!" whispered Raggedy Ann. "A mouse hole!"

Lying down on the floor, they looked inside.

Mother Mouse sat at her kitchen table, sniff, sniff, sniffing and wiping away her tears with a tiny napkin. The table was set, and Father Mouse and three little mousekins were all ready to eat, but there was no food, not a single scrap.

"It's no wonder she's unhappy!" said Raggedy Andy. "There's no food."

"Hello there," Raggedy Ann said. "We heard you sniffing, and now we can see why. Have you no food at all?"

Mother Mouse dried her eyes and came to the doorway with Father Mouse. "The mistress of the house keeps her kitchen very clean," she said. "We haven't been able to find so much as a crumb for the longest time."

"Marcella has learned such wonderful manners that she never drops or spills a thing," Father Mouse said. "That's good for her, but not for us."

Raggedy Andy asked, "What will you do?"

Mother Mouse started crying all over again.

"There, there," said Raggedy Ann. "Don't cry. We can help, and we *will* help. That's what neighbors are for!"

"Sure," said Raggedy Andy. "Marcella shares food with us, and we can share food with you. Just tell us what you need, and we'll march right down to the kitchen and find it!"

"This is so kind of you," Mother Mouse said. "I should give you a shopping list."

Raggedy Ann said, "I know! Let's make a picture list!"

Raggedy Andy found Marcella's crayons and a piece of paper. Soon they made a picture list of brown bread, Swiss cheese, red apples, yellow cake, and green peas.

The Mouse family waved good-bye as the dolls started to climb down the tall front stairs. Everyone made it down the stairs, except for Little Brown Bear. He lost his balance and went tumbling all the way to the bottom!

Little Brown Bear landed in a heap, but he wasn't hurt, because stuffed bears can't get bumps and bruises. Although he did not make enough noise to wake up Marcella's family, he did make just enough noise to wake up someone else!

Raggedy Ann and Uncle Clem helped Little Brown Bear to his feet. He picked up the list, then they all went around the corner and through the swinging door into the kitchen.

Uncle Clem said, "I'd forgotten that the kitchen is so large. This shopping trip is a big job!"

"Come on, Uncle Clem, help us move this chair to the counter," said Raggedy Andy.

Up on the countertop, Uncle Clem and Raggedy Andy opened the bread

box. Inside they found a nice, brown crust. After putting the crust in his kerchief, Raggedy Andy reached into a bowl of green peas. He scooped four big handfuls out and added them to his kerchief.

Little Brown Bear lifted up the glass dome over the cheese. Raggedy Ann reached under and chose a piece that did not have too many holes. She said, "After all, you can't fill a mouse's tummy with the holes in Swiss cheese!"

When Raggedy Andy got back down on the floor, he looked at the list and then looked around the kitchen. He said, "I don't see any apples, but here's a jar of raisins."

"Raisins are fruit and they're very tasty," said Uncle Clem.

Over in the corner, a very hungry puppy was watching. Fido liked raisins too.

Raggedy Ann and Little Brown Bear went hunting for some cake. It took a few minutes to get the icebox open, but inside was a pretty cake with pink icing. Raggedy Ann wrapped a piece into her kerchief. She said, "I think our shopping is all done!"

Fido licked his snout and scooted quietly out the kitchen door.

It was hard work to get the food up the stairs. Halfway up, Raggedy Ann said, "Shhh!" and everybody froze. It was Marcella's papa walking down the hall. They all stood very still.

"Whew!" whispered Raggedy Andy. "That was a close one!"

When they got to the door of the nursery, someone was waiting for them. Fido!

That naughty puppy pounced right at the bundle of cake in Raggedy Ann's hand, but Raggedy Ann was too fast for him. She ducked inside the nursery door, and Fido went sliding on the rug in the hallway.

"Quick!" said Raggedy Ann. "Get the food to the mice!"

By the time Fido got into the nursery, the dolls were only halfway to the toy chest. Mother Mouse cried out, "Hurry! Please hurry! All the food will be lost!"

Fido was coming fast, but all at once, Raggedy Andy had an idea. Peas! He turned around and emptied his kerchief onto the floor. Dozens of green peas rolled onto the wooden floor. The peas slipped under Fido's feet, and he went rolling like a bowling ball, right into his own basket in the corner!

Fido made a sad face—he didn't like peas at all.

"It's no fun to be hungry. Let's give him a little piece of cheese," Mrs. Mouse said. "There will still be plenty left for us."

Fido gobbled up his bit of cheese and wagged his tail.

Then everyone helped pick up the peas and gave them to the Mouse family. Some were a little squished, but they looked just fine to Mother Mouse and her hungry mousekins.

Father Mouse looked around his dinner table. His wife was happy, his children were eating, and they had plenty of food. He asked Raggedy Ann, "Is there anything we can do for you?"

Raggedy Ann thought a moment. Then she said, "I know Marcella's mama would prefer it if you and your family kept out of sight. And it would be nice if you would never nibble any holes in the sheets or quilts."

Raggedy Ann shook hands with Father Mouse, and she said, "This just goes to show that a good deed always leaves everyone better off than they were before."

All the little mousekins, filled up with second helpings of cake, agreed that this was true.